MERRY CHRISTMAS,
BIGELOW BEAR

MERRY CHRISTMAS, BIGELOW BEAR

DENNIS KYTE

DOUBLEDAY

NEW YORK   LONDON   TORONTO   SYDNEY   AUCKLAND

PUBLISHED BY DOUBLEDAY
a division of Bantam Doubleday Dell Publishing Group, Inc.
666 Fifth Avenue, New York, New York 10103

DOUBLEDAY
and the portrayal of an anchor with a dolphin
are trademarks of Doubleday,
a division of Bantam Doubleday Dell Publishing Group, Inc.

Library of Congress Cataloging-in-Publication Data
Kyte, Dennis, 1947—
Merry Christmas, Bigelow Bear / by Dennis Kyte
— 1st ed.   p.   cm.
Summary: During the excitement of the Christmas
season, Bigelow Bear neglects his best friend, a toy
truck named Ollie, but on Christmas Eve he
remembers the joys and responsibilities of
friendship.
[1. Friendship—Fiction.   2. Toys—Fiction.
3. Christmas—Fiction.]   I. Title.
PZ7.K993Bi   1990
[E]—dc20   89-25892   CIP   AC

ISBN 0-385-26522-0
ISBN 0-385-26523-9 (lib. bdg.)
RL:2.9

For Abiner Smoothie

Nestled in a forest glade blanketed with snow was the house of the Bear family—Mama Bear, Papa Bear, and their cub, little Bigelow Bear.

Bigelow Bear had many toys, but his favorite by far was a truck named Ollie. Ollie was more than a toy; he was a friend. Bigelow Bear and Ollie played together every day. They played red-light-green-light. They played toll booth. They played repair shop. They even made highways and bridges for Ollie to ride on. At night they would snuggle down to sleep in the same bed. Whatever they did together, it was great fun for Bigelow Bear . . . and Ollie, too.

Once, when Bigelow Bear had a cold and was too sick to play, Ollie dressed up as a doctor and brought his patient a sugar cookie and a glass of milk. Bigelow Bear smiled because he felt so

much better . . . and Ollie did, too! And when Bigelow Bear planned a picnic but it rained and rained, Ollie knew what to do. He brought the entire picnic indoors to Bigelow Bear's bedroom. It turned into a beautiful day for Bigelow Bear . . . and Ollie, too!

As Christmas drew near, Bigelow Bear helped Mama Bear decorate the house. He helped wrap packages and make holly wreaths. He even

helped make lunch, and when Mama Bear said, "Make sure you eat all your green beans," Bigelow Bear said, "And Ollie, too!"

igelow Bear helped Papa Bear gather the wood. He helped him shovel the walkways, and when they finished those chores, Papa said, "Okay, Grizzly Feathers, what do you say if before

we feed the ducks, I help you make some snow bears?" Bigelow Bear said, "Oh, yes! And Ollie, too!"

Later that evening Mama Bear said, "Tomorrow, Gramma Bear arrives for Christmas, and she is staying in your room with you. Make sure it's neat and tidy." Bigelow Bear was very happy, for he loved Gramma very much. That night, after playing with Ollie one more time, he cleaned his room, his closet, and even Ollie, too. When Mama tucked him in she said, "Sweet Fur, you did such a good job!" And Bigelow Bear answered sleepily, "And Ollie, too!"

Gramma arrived the next morning and moved into Bigelow Bear's room. She came with suitcases, satchels, boxes of all shapes and sizes, and shopping bags full to bursting. Gramma held out her arms and said, "Come over here and give me some sugar." Bigelow Bear ran over to her, climbed up into her arms, and gave her his sweetest bear hug, and a taste of his lollipop! Bigelow Bear loved his Gramma . . . and Ollie, too.

"Now, Fluffy Toes," Gramma said. "I think we should get to work on a gingerbread house." Bigelow Bear said, "Oh, boy, gingerbread! My favorite! Let's go, Gramma." He took Gramma's paw and led her to the kitchen.

Bigelow Bear had not said "and Ollie, too."
The toy truck very quietly followed them to the
kitchen and peeked in the door. Bigelow Bear was
having a wonderful time . . . and without Ollie,
too!

With all the Christmas fun and festivities over the next few days, Bigelow Bear didn't once play with his truck. Ollie didn't move. He just sat quietly in his garage. Then, on Christmas Eve, Bigelow Bear and his grandmother were getting dressed in their very best clothes. Gramma set her suitcase right in front of Ollie's garage—and Bigelow Bear didn't even notice.

riends and relatives filled the Bears' house. Candles flickered from tree and mantel. The air was sweet with the smell of fresh pine and sugar

cookies and gingerbread. Everyone gathered round and sang carols, and then sat down to a delicious dinner.

In Bigelow Bear's room, behind Gramma's suitcase, inside his dark garage, Ollie was alone. He could hear all the laughing and singing, but his heart was broken. His friend had forgotten all about him. First, Ollie closed his garage door, then he closed his eyes.

In the living room everyone was opening gifts.
Bigelow Bear got a tool set and a drum and a
complete cowboy outfit from Papa. He liked all his
presents, but it wasn't until Gramma came over to
him and said, "And a very merry Christmas to
you!" that Bigelow Bear's eyes opened wide. "Oh,
no!" he whispered to himself. "And Ollie, too!"

igelow Bear slipped away from the party and went to his room. Quietly, he got out all his blocks and went to work. He built highways and ramps, he built tunnels and bridges. He made narrow alleys and steep hills and splendid boulevards. Finally, with some leftover Christmas lights and tinsel, Bigelow Bear decorated this wonderland.

When Bigelow Bear had finished, he moved Gramma's suitcase and opened the garage door. Ollie looked up and slowly rolled out. The little truck looked around. He could not believe his eyes. Then Bigelow Bear said, "Merry Christmas, Ollie." Ollie beeped his horn and flashed his lights

and went for a ride
on his Christmas surprise.
It was a very special
Christmas for Ollie.

. . . and Bigelow Bear, too!